Where We've Been

For David,
fellow varsity onion ring
lover at GSU 94

Wm Greenway

William Greenway

Where We've Been

Breitenbush Books
Portland, Oregon

First Printing, October 1987
2 3 4 5 6 7 8 9

Library of Congress Cataloging-in-Publication Data

Greenway, William, 1947—
        Where We've Been

        I. Title.
PS3557.R3969W4   1987   811'.54   87-888
ISBN 0-932576-45-1
ISBN 0-932576-46-X (pbk.)

The author and publisher are deeply grateful to the National Endowment for the Arts, a federal agency, for a grant that helped make the publication of this book possible.

The publisher is grateful to Northwest Writers, Inc. for their assistance, and to the many individuals who contributed a gift to the press to assure the vitality and survival of the literary publishing program.

Text design by Patrick Ames
Cover design by Luba Yudovich
Cover art is from the frontispiece of the third edition of Pilgrim's Progress, adapted by the Media Center, Youngstown State University.

Breitenbush Books are published for James Anderson
Patrick Ames, Editor-in-Chief
Breitenbush Books, Box 02137, Portland, OR 97202-0137

Manufactured in the USA.

Acknowledgements

The author and publisher wish to thank the editors of the following publications where many of this book's poems first appeared:

Anthology of Magazine Verse and Yearbook of Poetry: Heart
Arete: Spider Drill
Blue Unicorn: Son and Heir
Cape Rock Journal: New Testament
Carolina Quarterly: The District of Looking Back
Croton Review: On the Bridge
Cumberland Poetry Review: Acclaim; Senior Year
Florida Review: Sea Change
Greenfield Review: Stress Test
Laurel Review: Nails; The Unities on North Avenue
Louisville Review: Another Marriage; Title
Manhattan Poetry Review: Atlantis; My Last Father Poem
Mississippi Review: The Book of Days; New Orleans, 1983; Custer
Montana Review: After the Fox; Scout
Negative Capability: The Life of the Mind
New Letters: Wedding
New Virginia Review Anthology 4: Milledgeville
Piedmont Literary Review: A Cat in Eden; Karma
Pig Iron: Five Clichés
Plainsong: Nothing's Been the Same Since John Wayne Died;
        The Teeth You Want to Keep; Men As Trees, Walking
Poetry: Heart; The Weaning; The Best Days of Your Life;
        Our Father Who Art on Third
Seattle Review: Visitation
Southern Poetry Review: The Last of the Sheridans
South Florida Poetry Review: A1A; Double Feature

CONTENTS

For Betty, and for my father, who never knew her

Some have also wished that the next way to their father's house were here, and that they might be troubled no more with either hills or mountains to go over, but the way is the way, and there is an end.

— *John Bunyan*

THE BOOK OF DAYS

If his life had been a novel, he'd have quit
reading long ago — characters
unbelievable, plot almost building, to fizzle
out halfway. A taunted weakling all
along, the hero, finally bearing serum to
a dying child, only falls asleep in
snow, not even real, but bills, paper. He
dreams of no back-slapping heaven of parents
and wives saying we never thought you
had it in you. Not even a dog comes
nuzzling through at the last, a wounded
wolf befriended in his youth. Maybe one
reader, the child he didn't know
he had, snowshoeing by. "Here," he gasps,
pressing the vial into a hand, "Nome.
Dying."

Bitter, numb already, you turn
into the wind. Your problem now.

HEART

He tells me I'm a risk —
he is small, blond, Mississippian. I trust him.
I am fighting my genes, he says, fighting
my father at fifty-two pulling off the highway
that had become a gray blur
trying to call to anyone from a phonebooth
while it broke in his chest, calcified, knobby
like an anklebone
and then again, over and over
in the hospital while doctors
ran up and down the halls trying to stop
that sequence of explosions,
that string of firecrackers.

You see yourself as glass
for the first time, transparent
shaken and fizzing, a bottle
of soda, and start watching
for potholes.
Or maybe you just learn to live
with a cart with square wheels
thudding in your breast
trying to carry whatever it is
there,
before it's too late.

This is how to become
old — worry only
about yourself.
So that if there come
bombs out of clouds
or lovers into rooms, saying
goodbyes, learn
how to cup your hand around it, as if
in a world of wind
there is this one candle
that must be saved.

THE UNITIES ON NORTH AVENUE

I pried them from baseball
bats, made them learn my
lines, sell tickets,
and we swept the red
dirt of our dank
cellar, strung a curtain
(shower), lit stolen
candles, called it
a tragedy.

Somewhere halfway through
the plot began to improvise
itself, a flock of script taking
wing, the spear (rake)
used on the wrong end.
A wooden sword cleft
the gray loaf of yellow
jackets who descended like
critics, the plastic curtain
sizzled black fog.

As I rounded the dogwood,
mother after me
with the rake/spear, I looked
back and decided to go
into poetry —

a frieze, tableau — Jimmy
Jacobs, his cape still
attached and whirling
muleta to Poochie
the dog, had delicate
blond Joe Nelson, who would
die at ten, in a headlock,
the basement behind spewing
ash and smoke, a sacked
city, bees swirling
around them like golden
snow in a crystal ball.

3

THE SOUTH UNDER RECONSTRUCTION

Waxing the car, I straighten up, old
in the back, rag in hand, remembering
suddenly for some reason Grant
Park, its deep hills, a zoo, cyclorama
with one slumped soldier half plaster, half
paint, his leg stumps blotted with flaking
blood, the world around misted with cannon
smoke, buzzards, burned pines arrowed in
the sides of Atlanta's red wound, invisible
choirs humming Dixie. Where my
mother took watermelons, busted
and ate them with either my father
or a sailor named Faris, where her
club met the time they hurt her
feelings and she dragged me out of the marble
pavilion to drive around awhile and cry
and they all hugged when we came back.
At reunions aunts wore membrane thin
flower dresses, gray buns, witches'
shoes, and uncles brown suits, snap
brim hats, badges and blackjacks. They
fried chicken, took black boys to
the icehouse, went to war, came home, died.
I can smell them like a seance — chicken,
sawdust, talcum, gunpowder. And car wax.
Did my parents drive there on
Sundays after the war? With me asleep
in a picnic basket or in her did we
polish an old car under the trees as if
we all had forever? I'll never know now.

DOUBLE FEATURE

Tonight they're running it again.
I ran in the back yard for days yelling
"Shane! Come back Shane!" after I
saw it, and just remembered where —
we'd leave the house to get there
before dark, cool at night in the summer,
and I cried quietly, mosquitoes and voices
in the back seat with me,
where I saw "The Thing"
huge and strong, vegetable, almost
unkillable.

Those were the good old days before
I got disconnected, like Alan Ladd only
far less fast or blonde,
more like James Arness, stranded and vicious,
bleeding dust when cut.

He wore a buckskin shirt and went
away because he loved his best friend's
wife. When they found him
under the ice, my hair
rose as they held hands and spread
out across the snow, making a hushed
circle of that shape, everything
I ever wanted to be inside.

THE LAST OF THE SHERIDANS

He laughed at her, saying
"But I'm already in hell."
She said, "All right," angry,
"you remember the cabin up
at the creek, when we'd all go and
Opal and Tommie would be there and all
the kids, and we'd go dancing every night?
Well that's what heaven is.
And we'll all be there," she shouted, "and you
won't. " He opened his mouth
as if she'd slapped him back
for all those times he'd hit
his only child with a butcher's hand
hard as a bed slat.

He was mean as a snake
when he was young, she said,
meaning drunk, beating up black
men in the ice house, braining a
cuckold with a ketchup bottle,
like his grandfather, the general
who said the only good Indian
was a dead Indian. I remember him first
a mile high, putting in
his dentures, a pink snail curled on
a row of pearls, sliding it in
and biting with a wet "chuck,"
looking down and saying
"You Scotchman, you."

He joined the next week as the choir
sang "Just As I Am," and mother,
crying, dragged me behind her
after him down the aisle, went
every Sunday after, driving slowly
home, the cars lined up for miles

on the two-lane road behind
his stories as if he didn't
hear the curses and the horns.

His black neighbor found him
in the yard, a small purple
stain at the white temple.
In the hospital clear tubes made sounds
like a straw at the bottom of a cup
and he held my hand
hard. When she touched him asking
"And who is this?" he snuffled out
words, eyes closed — "That's my
baby," his mouth said, empty, drawn
like a purse.

She still dreams about him
all the time — a little girl
again lying in the cabin at night she hears
a band far away playing the "Down Home Rag"
till the music dies to nothing,
and a fog begins to grow.
Somehow human at last
his face rises from the blue mist
of the night woods and calls her his baby
above the sound of rushing water.

THE LIFE OF THE MIND

"My, my. A body does get around."
Lena Grove

The summer Del
Shannon had a hit with "Runaway"
I was failing algebra, and my
grandfather told the story about slugging
his English teacher, jumping out
the window to run away and work
for the railroad, and eventually have mother
who had me.

Clark Goswick and I, on the last
day of school, before report cards
came in the mail, left for Daytona Beach
to work on fishing boats and marry
Cuban girls, but a cop caught us
after only two miles and four hours.
As we walked up the driveway, bleeding, our backpacks
solid with canned beans and bristling with fishing
rods, mother called from the porch
"Did they let school out early?"

When I fall across my desk
stricken, teaching
"The Road Not Taken" for the thousandth time,
an old salt on a dock somewhere
in Florida will be splicing
rope and telling yarns
to the dark children
of children.

SPIDER DRILL

There's this circle of orange
earth, the runner having to get
across. The coach slammed the ball
at me, who looked up and saw
Joe, the biggest and meanest in the third
grade, in the middle grinning. I still see my
running, in Christmas football pants, legs in
my mind moving faster than any
boy's ever, fly's wings, the ball
across my breast like a Bible.

On the other side, amazed, I looked
back to see him kicking dirt, hating
me with his teeth. I trotted to the
coach, handed him the ball like a star
and woke up face down, laughter in
the air like dust, clotting in my
mouth and eyes, coach over me, his
hand on Joe's shoulder, saying
way to go. Don't you *never* quit.

I replay it all the time, only
egging Joe on, blindside the kid
in the red pants. And more —
kick him while he's down, already
learning on the ground how there's
really only one
emotion: huge, sitting
in the center, all
the deadly sins, and virtues,
shame and love, hate and
pride, patience, greed, envy, even
revenge just
legs.

9

MEN AS TREES, WALKING

I learned early what that verse
meant, "For now we see as through a glass
darkly." My mother wouldn't buy me any
glasses because then I'd be a four eyes,
maybe even play in the band like the rest
of the pansies, or like my father, polishing
his lenses, head bent, hands
before his face as if
praying, no football
hero. Teachers tired of my leaning
in from the front row, chalk dust in
my hair, begged her in notes — like the blind
man in the Bible miracle, he sees men
as trees, and trees as lime
jello. Going out for passes, I was
lost like the end of the world when
everybody running sees the sky but me.
The coach threw his hat in the dust, "Son,
have you *ever* caught a pass?" I never
did, but when she gave in, let me have
my specs, it was like heaven, she even more
beautiful with wrinkles, people gross
as bears now limber as hickory, spare
as willows. And the trees, firmed up,
erect at last, were like emerald fish with each
scale whole and succinct, as if they would never
ever drop a leaf or a pass.

WEDDING

"Of men are you the most miserable; of women, I."

Medea

At the end she'd wake
to find him kneeling, head
on her lap. You're working yourself
to death, she'd say; he, if I
didn't have you to come home
to, I'd blow my brains
out. Thirty years they snarled, circled
a bone, sometimes me, some
days my sister, or money. If you
were a real man was on our coat
of arms, with never marry and
there is no happiness, *Nullus Felicita
Est.*

So I crave sorrow
like home cooking, need
to walk an aisle between
people dressed for it,
someone in white
robes and blood red emblems saying
words over it, the dead mailing
lead crystal, cut glass doorknobs
that don't fit for as long
as we both shall live.

[handwritten annotation: Son getting married?]

11

ANOTHER MARRIAGE

> "When you're lonely, praise the great lovers:
> the fame of their loving still isn't known enough."
>
> Rilke

When my father died my mother and I got
drunk every night, told each other
secrets, why I really left my wife,
that he cut the tips out of all her
bras, why he wouldn't go fishing all
those mornings, on the beach together
with a Polaroid while I slept. He left her
nothing, like that old joke, she laughed,
I've got money enough for the rest
of my life, if I die tomorrow. At the funeral
the preacher said I know how much you'll miss
him. How much I'll miss it, she said. He thought
she meant money, I thought the house she would
lose, the cooking and polishing she loved, but
she meant "it," like in novels and poetry about dead
lovers, how everything apparently ends
and you're left like her the day after, or him
the day before, swallowing tablets, stalling, pouring
foam on their burning hearts, both of them with enough
pain to last until they died, if they never did.

MILLEDGEVILLE

Castles of red brick in the rain, where my
"Granny" was, who thought the jets flew over
to take pictures of her clothesline of old
panties. Things she said made
the newspapers: "There," she'd
say, triumphant, "I *told* you they were
listening." From the fireplace. She could stay
there till death, or they could cut, a fifty
fifty chance, the first one. Downstairs
at night my father shouted against his
sisters. "Be it on *your* head then," they said.

He took us to see her, maybe the last
time, walking into old light
like yellow dust, lampshades, cracked green
walls, a room of sofas and steel bars.
She cried and called him Billy, a
child, "Take me home." I looked just
like him, her Billy. She wore a flimsy
flower print, for Sunday, black shoes like a
witch's, pointed bun of white hair. Somewhere way
off inside there was groaning, other crying.

Your parents always said, "If you don't behave
we'll send you to Milledgeville." Now I know
it was real, where Flannery O'Connor lived
with her mother and peacocks that called
like souls at dusk, remember how we
left her sobbing out "lobotomy" all
the way back down the hall, and the next
day, how it showed up in all the papers.

A1A

When we hit that highway in Jacksonville
a veil parted into an otherness five hundred
miles and ten days from August's red
dirt, scrub pine and football
practice, where my mother wanted
an athlete, and the coach wanted a state
championship. Skinny, timid,
I just wanted a stay of execution→*no football practice*
mixed of crushed bleached shells
and tar, blown and puddled with white
sand, running all the way down the coast just
behind one long dune, a green rampart
of sea oats and Spanish bayonet, Florida's
groves of water oak and olive even
at noon black, clustered, gnarled
Greek women whispering together, shade
caves of rusted cutlasses, eye patches, pieces
of eight falling spangled through twigs
onto the rooted gray sand carpeted with brown
scalloped leaves.
Fronds rattled all night in the salt wind
and neon palms blinked red, green,
red, green. Motels, Moorish, Tahitian, flashed
vacancy, their hula girls flickering hips back *←> neon*
and forth, the boardwalk over the beach
pouring pastel candy cotton, apple smells
and the heavy oil of hamburgers, onions,
corn dogs, boiled crabs. The screaming rides,
calliopes, drowned the hissing of the surf.
Every morning we drove, our car full
of coffee steam and canned milk, to the pier
stilted out over the green waves, its boards
strewn with translucent pink confetti, bits,
baby fingernails of shrimp shell and fish scale,
cobbles of lead sinkers crusted with salt, snarled
blond nests of old nylon line. We never caught
anything, but the whole ocean was always there

in case. And the fishing camp muffled with stained
sawdust, where we watched the throbbing boats
come in, throw colored bowed fish, sliding
in ice slime onto the dock, a shark
hanging on a hook, its gray bark
I reached out to touch with one finger,
a dark deep-sea pool with fins
gliding, giant turtle that raised its beaked
head to pshaw spray into the warm air above
where we walked across a wooden bridge afraid
we were falling through the cracks. It was
always there, summer after summer the
same until that last year riding in on the first
day, there all along, one thing too
many, a field bulldozed free
of palms and palmetto, where they practiced
football, the year I noticed that the blue
scrolled sign of our motel the Shangra-La
was spelled without an "i."

MY LAST FATHER POEM

Every Saturday he was bent
over the plastic voice of our
radio, the kitchen filling down
with the blue smoke of Camels,
oiled black curls falling
through the thin fingers that held
his brow. They were losing
again, where they taught about
flying, or building the planes.
But his Welsh father would only pay
for a seminary, until there was
mother, then the war, then me.
While I grew up in his father's house
he delivered telegrams, sometimes
on campus, came back and told me how
they all wore yellow satin jackets
and sliderules on their belts.
Or went and sat alone at night
above the grain yellow rink
he was tall enough to play in.
When only one college
would take me, tiny, far
from home, "No. That's real
good," he said. "They always
lose." Which meant to him
they only took the best.

TOO FAR TO WALK

Preachers spend half their lives in empty
churches, stopping by with their sons
on the way downtown to ball games. I hear his voice
far off, echoing, muffled in a small room below —
he's stained with violet ink, cursing
the mimeograph machine, or the folder
that mangles paper. In the pitiful
library, I look at Michelangelo's women,
cracked sepia breasts, plump
pears between their thighs, the finger
of naked Adam reaching out to God.

Summer janitor at thirteen,
I swept the hundred rooms of concrete
floors, metal chairs, shredded hymnals,
gray window light, the silence of stone.
On the block walls were palm
trees letting down spears
of light and Jesus drinking with the woman
at the well, walking on water, pointing
to his own heart. I dreamed of Brenda
Wilkie, underneath her white choir robe.

In my worst dreams I'm stranded
halfway between that red brick, city church
and home as the sun begins to set.
I can remember all the turns the car
used to make to get back into the suburbs,
but I'm walking and get lost, wander up
ever more branching roads into the hills past
the tangled cemetery where my grandmother
lies, into those neighborhoods where night
always falls on crumbled roads twisting
among houses with high
grass and all the windows dark.

ATLANTIS

This is the grave where I buried my
father, as if he could see blue
Kennesaw over there, where Johnston
dug in like a gentleman to have it
out, the big gundown, a duel. Sherman just
marched around him, cut him off, on
to Atlanta to burn. It grew back over, a
skin, a fur of honeysuckle and kudzu I could
grow in. Now each subdivision's
named something station or
landing, Civil War chic, new highways
squirming, red earth sucked to
the top and bleeding in the rain, that
K-Mart there in the hill's side as if
gouged by cannon, the boom of traffic.
Other than onion rings at The Varsity,
Brunswick stew at Old Hickory,
nothing beside remains, though I dream
my father, on summer nights, ringed
with shopping centers, sits in the cool
grass, feels the yellow ghost of honeysuckle, watches
flares and campfires up on the mountain
like fireflies, the besieged still holding
out, praying o
city that murders my prophets, o
blue general with fire
come home.

18

WHERE WE'VE BEEN

> "Tell us where you're going then, so when you get
> there, we can tell everyone where you've been."
> — a grandfather to his grandson in Crickhowell, Wales

I see the small, boy figure of Gwilym, my
grandfather, consumptive, climbing out
of Wales, over and past these gray, bouldered
hills, away from the black dust toward London
then onto a ship around the world. Pieces
are missing — how a cabin boy became
a cowboy in Australia, came to lay
rails in America, ending up
in Georgia's mountains, Methodist
circuit rider, why aeronautics engineering
wasn't good enough for Bill his son
who wanted to fly, that he must become
another preacher.

He rebelled too late, grounded
accountant marking the soaring of other
people's money, his crisp two's and
five's a flock of geese, flight
of arrows, checks down the long columns.
At forty he became a preacher so old and self
taught no church would have him, one voice
without a wilderness. Don't make my
mistake, he said, start early.

At thirty-five I come back
to Wales, coal mines gone, to
wonder if we're meeting, knowing
ourselves for the first time, strangers
sharing only a weak chin, small
mouth and name, or joined deeper
by an endless ability to hope
making all three of us lost together.

PIT PONY

There are only a few left, he says,
kept by old Welsh miners, souvenirs, like
gallstones or gold teeth, torn
from this "pit," so cold and wet my
breath comes out a soul up
into my helmet's lantern
beam, anthracite walls running,
gleaming, and the floors iron-rutted
with tram tracks, the almost pure
rust that grows and waves like
orange moss in the gutters of water
that used to rise and drown.
He makes us turn all lights off, almost
a mile down. While children scream
I try to see anything, my hand touching
my nose, my wife beside me — darkness palpable,
velvet sack over our heads, even the glow
of watches left behind. This is where
they were born, into this nothing, felt
first with their cold noses for the shaggy
side and warm bag of black
milk, pulled their trams for twenty
years through pitch, past birds
that didn't sing, through doors
opened by five-year-olds who sat
in the cheap, complete blackness listening
for steps, a knock. And they
died down here, generation after
generation. The last one, when it
dies in the hills, not quite blind, the mines
closed forever, will it die strangely? Will it
wonder dimly why it was exiled from the rest
of its race, from the dark flanks of the soft
mother, what these timbers are that hold up
nothing but blue? If this is the beginning
of death, this wind, these stars?

NEW TESTAMENT

I'd never be that
way, white-haired and prophetic,
stern as Solomon, with full pockets.
He'd bend over and out would fall
pens. He'd pick them up and his
notebooks would drop, then
the tiny green Bible. He'd
bend to pick them up and out would fall
pens. Good night alive, he'd shout,
almost a saint except for
the squatting mimeograph machine,
his own pockets,
and his son.

And mother liked James Dean, so for years
it was easy — long hair, leather
jackets, guitars, anything
he wasn't. Until things began
to fall. I made sure they were
cigarettes, small airline
liquor bottles, prophylactics,
switchblades.

Graying, I bent groaning today in the new
asphalt street to tie my
hushpuppy — the ball of ice
cream tilted out, then the ball
point pens, then another ragged
poem. I stood with an empty cone
in the center of the littered black
street and said God
damn him, and tried to mean it.

VISITATION

I'd been there before, knew when I stepped
off the plane, a hick, into the air-conditioned
air. There was smog, yes, but something
else, a tang — eucalyptus, burning
brush in the sun, a cool musk blowing
off a northern sea that the folds of the desert
hills poured into, congealing like lava. The freeways,
bald and ugly, rolled themselves by blue
waves flecked with the jade pods of kelp, cold
brine and a beach the color of flesh. At evening
crepe myrtle, mimosa, hibiscus, frangipani trailed
tentacles, scarlet cupped, and the scent of warm
sage, shades of conquistadors in pewter,
boulevards of heron-crested palms leaned
in, all my movies, Saturday matinees, confused —
Tom Mix zinging bullets off of boulders just
over the hill from the beast with a million
eyes, giant ants and the San Andreas
fault, a lavender stain of sand sliding
quietly south by San Jacinto like a mountain
of the moon. The radio sifted the air
for a song, "Riders On the Storm," the notes
flickering stars above Mount Palomar,
a crowd with candles shouting jump
to someone on a ledge, white-robed
congregations at night in blind canyons, lights
of L.A., a pond of phosphorescent motes seen
from mountains of coyotes, howling.

I told no one my vision — the earth, dirty
dangerous and holy — except once:
a group laughing on the beach,
brown, wet with oil and floured with sand.
They loved my accent and made me say it over
and over, like a cowboy star of the thirties
or something from another world.

CAIN

That old cracked couple down the street
could be Adam and Eve, still, the way
they tend their fat acre, or the Poe
story, keeping death out — ramparts of
azalea, jonquil pikes, corner spumes
of white dogwood. Maybe death will *never*
win, their rich thumbs sprout, grass
swarm over the mound of grave. So why
are they afraid? They see it as smut, a mildew,
something that shows up in
place of the milkman, sniffing all
the color from their flowers, slobbering
over the jade shrubs, peeing a
stain in brown runnels of blight through
the veins and arteries of their tough
St. Augustine. They even keep its runners
in, stack their gritty borders with concrete
block lest something park and watch.
From their glass breakfast porch they
hold each other, shaking free
fists at it, the way they cross to the
other side when they pass my rented yard
with its plastic chair among the dead
leaves, broken limbs and bicycles
in the shadow of the shaggy copper
beech that has been rust from the beginning.

ADVENT

On the road past Lake Serene, someone
has torn down the bridge out
sign, and while pickups doze in the blacktop
lots of shouting south Mississippi
churches, we drive on across concrete
spillways, our tires hushed in water,
looking at the mansions and the leaves
until we come to the new bridge of broken
white wafers down in the red gorge
the lake seeps through to become a stream
again.

Since we have to stop
anyway, we get out to look for pine cones
to fill Christmas baskets. Fresh
fallen from the storm last night they're
hard, unopened, pink as flesh, long
thin pineapples. Like crusts of bread
they lead us along the bluff, layered
like orange desert cliffs, and around
to the lake, the shallow end away
from the yachts and boat docks, to where
mud has cracked in autumn's low water.

Now a grid of slick gray tiles
furred with evergreen lies beneath
clear water only inches deep. Mussels,
fat brown parabolas etched with rings
like trees, bubble between the cracks.
On the shore, in sand, we see tracks of
raccoon, watching us from the pine
dark woods, and the shells they've
beaten open with both paws and left
in the sun to be pearl butterflies
everywhere. Out in the lagoon, navy,

rippled with the cold north wind, are
thousands of logs, stumps, each
knobbed with turtles.

Back at the car we thump
the pine cones into the trunk
and open a mussel, part the thin
lips to show us something inside —
wet, soft, curled like a small
tongue of glycerin and amber.

NAILS

I'm taking apart a packing
crate in the back yard, building
a bookcase of the pieces, hoping
my wife will come back and see
what I was, though I've told her
often enough. It must be the smell
of pine, the scraps we burned
in barrels, shivering, climbing in the
morning out of the purple shadow up
on that beached skeleton of yellow
bones, the heaped mud below us flecked
with nails, into the parallel gold
bars of sun above the trees, slippery
rime on the boards, glistening
snail tracks, until the sun
thawed it to damp the wood a shade
darker, pulpy as stale bread
to the nails, ringing slightly when
you let the hammer do the work, if
you're good, just lifting it
to fall, going in deep with one
blow, the boards blonde as women, lime
streaked with grain, powdered with the fine
dust our saws give off into the morning
like pollen. Splinters, and drops
of blood like blots of rust. Insects
grow louder as the sun rises. We
throw aluminum cans of water
underarmed, lateralled like
footballs, silver bullets twirling, throwing
off curls of the water that tastes
like sugar, metal cold in the throat.

She comes around the house bringing lemonade
and stays to watch. I begin to tell the story again

as things start to bend and tear.
I begin to sweat, saying
I used to…
do this…
for a living
but my story, like this project,
is going nowhere, and she yawns.
Your stories go nowhere
too, I say, the famous
England trip, hiking in the Rockies,
the alleged year you spent as a waitress, you,
who've broken every dish in the house.
But she just laughs and goes
back in.

Now the nails straighten again
by themselves and sink into the wood
forever, shining, hidden.

A CAT IN EDEN

They make fun of our spoiling her, felt
catnip toys, canned escargot, a tiny
wine list.
But her forerunner got hit chasing
squirrels in the street because we wanted her
to be free, happy, the one we raised
by hand with a doll's bottle she sucked
and chewed, her blind mouth brimming
with evaporated milk. She made a nest
in my hair at night, and I had fleas
for months, long after she was dead.

This one wears a harness and leash
she drags around the yard all day
like a small, abandoned sled dog.
Most of the time she just sits, miserable,
humiliated, as if she's being forced to wear
a hat. We keep a broomstick
handy for dogs and snakes.

They only live ten or twelve years
anyway, at the most,
but we want to bury her wrinkled,
arthritic, bored,
though she sits for hours thinking, scheming
of a breakout, dreaming
of mice and trashcans,
hating our guts.

We could care less. We don't
philosophize
anymore — we just
patrol.

SENIOR YEAR

"But I don't love *him.* I love
you." I turned to see her
within the morning shade of a small
tree, standing as if she'd just
stamped her foot, arms crossed, holding
together her trembling yellow dress.
His head was bowed. They were being
miserable, but oh what
misery. The butler, I walked
on, hadn't heard a thing.

Though it's still warm, fall
has begun, the sun already
slanting in the afternoon, flaring
the brick buildings orange and gold, one
or two leaves turning early, here a dot
of russet, mauve. The evenings are
sentimental, smells of woodsmoke and something
invisible just beginning, blooming
too late. Hearing winter, sick
cats push at my window tonight
to be fed, broken-winged birds
struggle out in the dark, fish with
eyes hooked sink, their scales releasing
the summer moon. Wounded things
begin to ache before it snows and all
the books I've ever read weigh tons,
and that's outside the mind.

HIGH RISE

I've never been this far above
the earth as now returning to the city
of my birth. Far off to the south out
the plate glass window of the fifty-seventh
floor, the red brick project where I was
conceived, across the street the college
my father couldn't afford, the jade pool
of football field where I sold cokes. How
appropriate it would be to die here on this
brief and single visit above it all, remember
fires on TV, hotels like this burning like
matches, all the smoke alarms and sprinklers
no comfort. I imagine air bags like biscuits
down in the street, if I could hit one, aim
straight enough, have the courage to
jump and live, or die. Before sleep I try
to pray, or imagine catching passes, but feel
no earth beneath my feet, only the hum
of this tower in wind, and dream only of
falling. As I dress to go home, dawn
reddens the city like a dig in Pompeii so that I
could step out into it, kneel and brush away with one
finger, from the streets between cinnamon
roofs, red dust to find within one brick doll's house
my mother, still curled on her first bed afraid
that if she gets up the seed won't
take. I pull from my coat the long
blonde hair of my wife and remember
Lawrence's mother, how her one white strand floated
up the chimney into nothing. From my pants
I brush the short gray hairs of my own
head, the pale banded filaments of cats.
They all float down to the floor
of the fifty-seventh floor. Outside
clouds are forming, coming toward me as if
I were one of them, one of those souls in old
prints that fly up like clouds out of the dead,
or the just beginning to be.

TWO-DREAM SONNETS

I.

I was a child again.
In the park a girl
with blonde hair watched only
me. I could tell she loved me.
Dream children are lamed so
they can't follow you home,

but I got lost, ankles in
sawdust when the barker stopped me, towering
above, pointing to the tent side painted
with the giraffe people, the woman rose
tattooed, then the green tiny
earth in a blue pond circled by some
kind of blond bird on a string. Blood
red caption: Mandolin Music in Space!

II.

You flew my kite. Blood
red silk formed a rose,
the green stem a tail.
It nodded in the wind all day,
a lily tethered in a stream
I watched until dark when

passion made us grow — lying
in grass we strained lips, limbs like
giraffes for leaves, twined
necks, became
a tower on the hill. Silence haunted this desire,
though ghosts, wind, and the wings
of birds whispered.

ESSAYS

They are splayed in front of me
like a new hand of cards, thirty,
each bending to the topic, the major
problem facing college
freshmen, and I wonder what
on earth I would write, probably
remember first the second
semester, chosen to room with the one
they all adored, filling
the shower with guitar chords
and steam, sitting up on the gravel
roof and watching cars from the late
shift at the quarry go home, running
naked to steal honeysuckle from
the dean's bush and piling it high
on the desk we never used, the others
coming by just to smell it, closing
back the door without a word until
it faded, brown tendrils limp, jade
leaves dusty, the window open in the spring
afternoon blowing scent and cream flowers
down the hall. Singing hits all night,
"The Bright Elusive Butterfly of Love,"
"Did You Hear the Lonesome Whippoorwill,"
sleepers beating time on our walls, the house
mother almost crying, you've got to stop singing
that bird song. We laughed at her
and swaggered off through half a year.

But of the first I would write only of
my father leaving me there, a room
in a house so dark I dreamed
only of death, hiding in the basement
of the dorm, and then home at
Christmas, riding to the hospital, moaning
over and over, not she doesn't
love me anymore, but "alone"

32

over and over, surprised,
as if this was all I'd learned
or how people only love the people
they won't let themselves have,
or that from out of where you cut your
arms what there is of you to hurt
passes forever like blood leaving
white tubes that don't need anything
just to go on writing how I somehow
still sit each night on top of that house
watching the night shift wind like pairs
of stars down that hill, around
that house that is alone, on the hill
that is still alone in that country
on this same earth that always
hangs in the night until it's time
to hand these papers in and go home.

NATCHEZ TRACE

Four hours from the city
is a way through the first forest.
Within a tunnel of trees
moccasins and oxen hooves
walked it down until the land around
makes walls laced with roots.
Paved with leaves the road
dips to cross streams pebbled
like separate trails we walk
in all directions, barely
wetting our feet. We
see raccoon tracks two
by two, the twin blades of shy
deer spoor, red squirrels boring
deep into the boles of trees turning
gold, fogged blue in the morning
with the smoke of the hardwood
fires of our waking, shivering
to pack up and go.
Tomorrow the leaves will be one shade
brighter, changing all the cold night
for us, at home, angry again.

IN AUTUMN

We were camping. He
came out of the woods, thin, scarred,
shivering as he walked. We fed him
spaghetti, salami, stale
bread he ate till almost dead and buried
the rest, knowing winter, how
no one comes to sleep by the lake.

We found wood to burn in a grove
of oak, cut and left to rot.
He stayed in darkness, beyond the fire.
Headlights came at midnight, halloing.
He cowered as if the voice were over him
with a stick. We kept
quiet, hiding, but the pickup
came down, asking about a liver-spotted
hound. Seeing the twelve-gauge, we said no
dog here.
When we left he ran after us
partway up the road.

Today it is full winter, gray and drizzling, even
up on that acre of rotting trees, on that
lake where no one comes but hunters
calling home their dogs.

SCOUT   Real

I stalk the nature trail
trying to see deer
or even a rabbit.
The leaves still wet
I creep like moccasins
when suddenly I hear
something coming
on the trail ahead.
Had I a rifle
I'd have shot a young
doppelgänger, red bandanaed.
He says as we pass
you think you're alone out here?
You've got a surprise coming
about a hundred yards up.

About a hundred yards up
a hundred boy scouts are waking,
screaming, chasing through the woods
casting lures into trees,
burning bacon.
A scoutmaster, mounty cap crooked
on his head, sits
wrapped in a khaki blanket
his face sleeping in his hands while
green and yellow tents sag everywhere,
radios twang, and clumsy
fires pour up blue smoke.
I used to beg my mother
to let me join, go on these trips,
but she thought I was too frail.
Old as the scoutmaster
I am finally learning to camp,

Danté
Inoser

36

dreaming in my tent of grizzlies,
burning my fingers,
chopping my feet.

I see one trying to fill
a plastic jug with a two-handed pump.
He looks alone here, not a member
of anybody's gang.
I hold the jug like a
scoutmaster would while he
pumps and tells me about the hike
they took yesterday so long even
my feet begin to ache.
We fill the jug, look
at his blisters,
tighten up his tent and then
sit down by his smudge of fire.
Glad of the company
he offers me black bacon
and a slice of toast
spread with cold butter
and ashes like pepper.

When I leave he goes to show
the way I'd lost, pointing
from the fork we come to
and is still there, smaller,
standing in a spot of sun
at the first bend before I go
into the deepest part of the woods.

ON THE BRIDGE

Fishing, our lanterns hung just
above the slick black water make
holes filled with fish, squirming
eels in a barrel of yolk.
Offshore, the oil rigs crouch,
steel mosquitoes, their needles
syphoning out the long dead
and fishing boats inside the reef
illegally, running lights off,
use the moon instead rising
red and swollen through air sifted
with volcanic ash.
Dolphins in the bay circle and charge
again and again with ivory teeth
into the shoals of trout
busy snapping minnows and shrimp
on the surface, and sometimes
our hooks that
snag them up to beat
off their scales on the loose
gravel of the bridge
with the bloody moon rising
over hooks and nets everywhere, things
leaping into hoops of light appearing
almost glad to die.

AFTER THE FOX

Each day they try to hold the island
that's moving, folding, crawling like an octopus
back to mainland. Finger paring, it's dissolving
to the invisible quick. Bulldozer noise is a
surf, choppers hover with the gulls.
The beach is fished out this year from
mud-dredge and a hard freeze. Up here
on the night bridge fewer than ever come
to lanterns pasting a jade ball on the tidal
river, hanging mosquitoes for minnows, then shrimp
flipping for trout — first the first of their
flash, then shades weaving the falling tide, .
someone down the bridge, their bending down
face, reflected yellow moon, whispering there
they are, here rising, here sperm
squirming in a yolk, snapping foam. They
hover, seem to be swimming like hounds ran,
back when there were foxes, if you caught in
helicopter searchlight their streaming from
the spool, forming, flattening to take a
hedge, thinning like water through rocks,
spinning filaments through trees, resuming
the skein on the other side, not running but
riding land-flow beneath. This is how they
hold the tide, though the rigs offshore
flare their gas-burn wells, illegal black-boats
drag their trawls, how they will come back
every night to our lamps for years
even when there is only one left
or one light left to come to.

REUNION

It's New Orleans but it isn't.
There's no heat, no black mud levee,
just cool jade grass declining
to the clear Mississippi, cobalt
blue flowing so shallow over sand
that we can wade across.
And trees everywhere, but no houses,
only small grocery stores in the groves
of water oak, in the shade of Spanish moss
with formica tables where old friends
can sit and drink beer
who haven't seen each other for years.
Some of us are even dead
so that we could easily cry
about this last chance
except we're shy and speak only
of how much weight we've lost,
how good we still look.

We know we are only dreaming,
have met in a nexus of time and night,
so why, as we talk, explain, apologize, do we
smile with a secret, as if
summoned to this heaven by
our need for each other again
as if one of us sent out a call?
By the river on the night of the twenty-fifth
and don't be late.

CUSTER

"Buffalo Bill's defunct."

You were born into it, certitude, like the air
you came into, waiting to breathe, the lemon
color of your hair, the teeth you assumed.
Everything after fell in line — a white horse
high-stepping to "Gary Owen," a wife
who needed you like bread, the eyes
of a country. You knew — looking
at women, drawing a bead, or an ace —
but unsatisfied, itchy, there was still a catch,
a skip, still in the breast, a
stutter, priming your heart, turning
the head at odd moments, expecting
a door, something to enter, go through.
And then you saw your first Indian
and finally showed that famous smile
everything around you dead.

ACCLAIM

I've been there when five
have tied a game, pistol
hands going off, revolution,
emotion rising to the dome like fog, tear
gas, red ants swarming.

Only tenors and athletes get that
instant backwash, echo of greatness
slapped from a cliff face
back, the ball, high C
going through touching nothing
at all.

What about Keats then, just
after, say, the Grecian
Urn, nobody, nothing but a sagging
candle, there that late. Old
silence. Or maybe the sound when
silence is shifted one cog over
by a poem, as though you'd turned
the wheel left, went right
and for a second
where are you?

As if the wrought-iron bench,
beneath you in the sunny side-
walked, bird, bicycle, new
leaved, skates and flowered
park, its lion paws set
in warm concrete that twines steel
tap roots down, were,
by a single thought, just
ever so slightly
moved.

OUR FATHER WHO ART ON THIRD

"After all, he said to himself, it is probably
only insomnia. Many must have it."
A Clean, Well-Lighted Place

I stopped praying years ago, learned how
to think instead of love, or the icy mountains before
death, green fields beyond. Now I need
a quiet god, not to make the heart rattle,
a golf ball in a cup. Baseball fits best,
almost as if designed in sleep — the pickoff, brush
back, squeeze, suicide squeeze, stealing. It's no
heaven — it's here: slick skin and stitches of the ball
in hand reminding me of Ebba St. Claire, Atlanta
Cracker catcher built like crossed trees, showing us
how to throw, the ball an egg in the knotted
roots of his fingers. If he never made it, how
can we? Yet I wear before sleep the welts
and wrinkles of a glove, dream hand, grip the bone
handle of a Louisville Slugger, slap clay
from my spikes and go toward the dark as to
home, playing for the bunt, the sacrifice.

BEFORE THIS HAPPENED, GOD

"God is love."

Before this happened, God
was something inside, familiar, warm
as an organ. Now it's far
away, white-haired and thunderous,
a dirt dam I plug stormy nights
on my knees that sickness won't
balloon into death, that accidents
swerve and carom around us, the vessel
in my wife won't burst, my heart
get sulky and tired, the wrong woman
show up.

All good tragedies are those of
love, and therefore God, inside of us
yet still outside, like dreams
of dams bursting overhead, tornadoes
circling, things, rising from dark
swamps, red-eyed, taloned, coming closer.

FIVE CLICHÉS

We see her in K-Mart housewares
buying an oh god no, and look away
fast, one of those freak accidents, the way drunken
cowboys pass out in the middle
of a west Texas prairie night, the sun
spotting their bondoed pickups neatly
on the rails until the once-a-week express
slices their dreams in half. But this is trying
to be art, this poem, imitate her life
better than it's been imitating Modern
Romances — twitching a blonde coed across
the path of her lying hound of a husband.
So now, just a little too late to start
over, she'll step out of her house of new
kids onto her new K-Mart
doormat, and her own sidewalk's
banana peel will skid her
into the street to kiss the Mack
truck that's been coming down through the language
for years. I bet they find one of her pink jogging shoes
almost a mile away.

TITLE

Harry, Hilary, John, I get
the names all wrong, say them for
good morning, see their smiles
sag and disappear. Later I know
I've called them wrong, as if
I didn't know or care. And how
can I go back and make it up, make it
good? Tell them what is wrong and always
was, how often I hear fuses shorting
and snapping, see only a question
mark of smoke puff from a gray box
on the house's white side, how it hangs
and blows away in morning wind
into green, the spring trees
lime-green and thick? How I dream, names
changed, Philip my wife losing her fine
dark hair, Mary my mother, bearded, or
Don with her breasts, my dead father who comes
tired to me each night, the one I
embrace saying lover, friend?

THE DISTRICT OF LOOKING BACK

I've seen too many, interviews
where they remember exactly forever
what they were doing when it
happened. I had just opened a)
the door b) a beer c) my Bible
to Deuteronomy when I heard the
explosion/growl/roar like a freight train,
thud like thunder shaking the house.
Where were we when Kennedy was shot?
Where was Sheilah Graham but in the kitchen,
Scott standing by the mantelpiece, taking
out a carton of milk, lighting
a cigarette. So I keep trying this way to live
as if each moment were the last — now I'm
putting on my shorts. I had just put on
my shorts. The way you run a tape forward
to the good parts, what came just before and
who cares what just after. There's a part of
Jamaica so rough all the men wear their black
sharkskins striped with the slick ebony of razor
welts. They call it we no send, you
no come from the days they rode back
to back, two
to a horse, the front one always saying how
he heard the thump, then the shot itself just
as he'd turned the bend. "But all I saw was where
I was going. And the poor
bastard never even knew where he was, only where
he'd been." And maybe this is the way we keep
leaving each day, each moment, as if we'd never
been, except for the one where we must
stay, like getting off a train at a station that will be
that second forever, for us and for the someone else
left to remember exactly what they were doing
when they turned and we were gone.

OBJECTS IN MIRROR ARE
CLOSER THAN THEY APPEAR

For a long time I kept dreaming
my wife died suddenly. She'd step
on a board that would crack and down
she'd go, getting smaller, my heart
with her, mouth still trying to say
even the first syllable of her name.
I would never know it was coming — we'd
be in England walking a castle wall, she'd
step out on some scaffolding to rescue
a kitten before I could stop her. Or onto
a slick green stone in the river above
falls. And then she really almost did, one
second fishing by me in the sun, then
the emergency room, the doctor saying
something's certainly going on in there.
Inside you laugh like a bad step on a gravel
roof. Then a step to right yourself
that doesn't hold. But you were gone from
the first, that slight sway from dead
center to where gravity is waiting — Wallenda
on the high wire in the wind, dropping his
pole then himself like an ice cream cone, the space
shuttle, another bottle rocket. Or you try to split
the difference between two semi's slamming like
doors — the silence while you ride limp as a rag
the crest of a wave, watching the spot where
you'll hit, heart beating fastest just before
it stops. Movies make it almost leisurely —
the bullet smacks, you reel, wobble, spin,
stagger, fall in someone's arms. They hold
your head while you name
names: trap door, banana peel, frog tongue.

BURIAL

What is it after all but a
judgment, a pronouncement? Someone has to say
"He's dead," and someone always does, but
if they're still here, that is, the body, then
they're still here. Eyes closed, perhaps,
heart stopped, of course. But what if no one
said it, made that decision? We would
notice a lapse of words, a slight
slumping of the body, a pause
in the air of the room. We would
go on talking until, tired, we
went home, calling their house out of habit
for years. If we badly needed to know what
only they knew, like the name of an
obscure actor, or a book, we
could go to them and ask. Until it got too
ugly. Eventually, every thought of them would trip
on the certainty — that where they were
there was still silence. We would stop
going, stop calling.
This is death then. Not them, not their
decaying, as we all do, or their
thinking deep in the eyes as if quiet
for some *reason,* but only
us, our giving up.

SEA CHANGE

When the doctor told me
I went to the bathroom
sat down and wept on the tall
toilet for the sick and dying.
Wept. Crying's for babies, mashed
thumbs, not for the world like
a bruised grape or a fisted
eye. The tile room filled slowly up
with grief, a roar in
my ears, submarine. But as low
as I was, you were still below
me, sedated, sleeping, or talking
with eyes closed, beyond
pain, sinking, wrapped
in white, your hair a coral fan
on the pillow. All I wanted
to tell you, serious, desperate from that
height, was my love and guilt, something you,
growing deeper, darker, already
didn't need, the vein into
that pale, floating arm a tether
to your new current,
leaving me to drown for years.

SON AND HEIR

You came uninvited, a stark
and slimy, inconvenient thing
we couldn't throw out,
two romantics as we are.
So we raise you in this sty,
this poverty without hope
of prospects or college
only words and food from cans.
You'll hate my guts,
I knew that from the beginning.
Maybe you'll even be the one
to finally punch me out, split my lip
when I pitch a fit, screaming
at your mother. You'll yell
you selfish pig, and I'll turn
and play my ace, saying
coldly, levelly,
I never wanted you.
But for now I walk you
back and forth at 2 A.M.

Angry at this intrusion on my
liquor, late movies, and poems
I shake you a little too hard.
But you don't cow,
you just wrinkle in your red face
and blow a scream
back at me, already letting
into my mouth
the bitterness of blood.

NOTHING'S BEEN THE SAME
SINCE JOHN WAYNE DIED

My world isn't hers, skin
like mocha she climbs into
each morning, air pouring
through her throat clear
as creekwater, no line where
brown legs slide into
silk shorts. She's my student
but I'm in class now, aerobics,
flunking in a room of convex
mirrors and dumbbells, though
she's patient, pities me, the
sounds I make for air. It's
hopeless as a dancing bear, Disney
hippo in a tutu, a friend's
father. She wants to pop
candy in my mouth when I do
something right. Cigarettes
smell like burning celery, liquor
is shellac, her heart has a slow
beat and sticks to it, she can bench press
me. I sort of pity *her,* daughter
I never had, how far she has
to go, how dirty and heavy.
But she's perfect now, and even
her hard music gets under my
fat, sets my frog leg jumping
in jean stores.
She's working hard to get me young
I'm aging her fast
and three times a week
we keep meeting here.

IT'S WHAT YOU SAID YOU WANTED

My old fishing buddy calls to ask
if I still want that skull, that a guy's
in town selling them at a plastic
surgeons' convention. Forty to two
hundred dollars each, depending on
how many teeth are left unbroken.
He buys in India but will have to stop
in August, a new law. I tell him
no, that that was when I thought death
was cute, like Sarah Bernhardt, with her Hamlet
prop and sleeping every night in
a coffin, before all those hours in
the hospital doing crosswords, afraid to read
a novel in case I ran across words like
"love," or "alone," or "wife." Before she
opened her eyes and said it looks like you're finally
going to be free. Or before I quit
smoking and started jogging because the man
in the next room, gross and wheezing, was swelling
every day, slowly exploding like something already
dead in the sun. Before I found out I was happy and
always have been. Pretty soon, my friend says,
all skulls will be plastic, and we talk
about fishing again in the Gulf, how
we're going to stand waist deep in that jade
water, how we're going to bust those trout, really
put ants on them, how we're going to let them go.

THE BEST DAYS OF YOUR LIFE

All those commercials pushing zest, out
lusting each other for life. Soon they'll come
on holding a can and have a fit, as if last
second a million beings hadn't died.
There. Another legion, souls fizzing
from cancers like tire air, an extra
thousand little brown balloons gone
from lands where the dirt is cracked
like lips. Next second or the next a billion
bugs will conclude, applauded from
this life, round off incarnations, they
hope, fireflies shush into dark like matches
in water, small animals furred and shelled just
pop on the highways, champagne
corks on the edge of a new
year that's always happening, interstates
of hearts stopping, seizing black engines
out of oil. Slugged bodies falling down
the sky, bulldozed, floating up, blood
vessels puffing and splitting, but you'd never
know by watching television, which is why
they talk about life being such a wonderful
thing, and it is, at least mine is.

THE TEETH YOU WANT TO KEEP

After I hit thirty, I found
I began looking forward to it, even
the cartoon lion saying floss
only the teeth you want to keep.
He tells me they use it to string
agate beads it's so strong. The needle
is somewhere in my head, the cobra
cyclops peering at me over
his shoulder, war of the worlds.
The pain hides like a pin
in a haystack in the next
county, but will come back later
with drums. I give off dust like
a quarry and his fingers smell
like Dachau. Outside, air comes
into my mouth half cold, half
hot, and my ringing right ear
hears me from across the room
thanking him around the oyster
of my tongue, lisping that while pain
is good, this is better.

BODY AND SOUL

A long time we've known
each other. I worried how
thin you were, how chalky
soft your bones, so ugly, sharp
nose, tiny mouth like a carp's, weak
chin. We grew apart because
you couldn't keep up.
But you did keep calling, sometimes
drunk, long distance, your whining
bad lungs whistling, another sore
that wouldn't heal, a new growth
ballooning, your heart heavy as a black
anvil in a fruit crate, twinges
like blue thorns on cold vines
lacing through your arms, in
your ears the noise of crickets
in dry grass. I listened to your fear
just the way I did when I cared.
But now your calls wake me like stabs
in the dark. I turn on the lamp to tell you,
before hanging up, turning back
off the light, if you're going to go,
go.

NEW ORLEANS, 1983   *Reincarnation*

I've been there. In another room a woman
laughs, but the lime-green
fields are rice, the black clouds
monsoons coming across the Bay
of Bengal whipping orange
saris along the plain of beach, a
temple ruined in jade, vines
strung with red monkeys, stones
of steps going down into
the brown Ganges, white cattle
in the streets, golden curry, woman's
violet lips, that forehead spot, third eye.

A boy, stinging their flanks
with a bamboo pole, drives water
buffalo at dusk, a man walking
with a smiling girl traces
something with his hands — a passion, a
memory: gray moss above a black
river, snakes with the marks
of diamonds, red dust, cotton.

KARMA

In my other life, I stayed
up all night, in charge of the moon
in the clearing, where the sticks
got up and
joined hands and
danced.
I had a crown of clover and baby's breath
and sweet minions
and I presided sitting on a soft
mushroom, drinking moonshine
from an acorn cup till dawn
when I was put to snore between the roots
of a great tree.
This went on for three hundred years
and I died.

I woke up human, and Baptist, in Atlanta, Georgia —
which shows you what can happen
when you don't pay attention.

STRESS TEST

The Indians say, it's a good day
to die — grass smelling like
watermelon, wind blowing yellow
flour. I sign a pink
tissue that will swear if I drop
dead it's no one's fault but my
own, unsaid the mountains of cigarette butts
and liquor bottles, the doctor pitying
me like a sinner — he's brown
and spare as a monkeyor
astronaut. Young girl-jocks in
ballet tights paste their soft
leeches to my chest, and the treadmill,
narrow as a beam, starts flowing, waits
for no man. Out flows the plastic
paper of my every second, peaks,
and valleys when the body pauses,
debates like a fist whether ever
to open again, pull in like a swimmer
before the breast's stroke. Soon
the leather river has beaten me, I'm
winded. "Are you through," she says.
They wrap the tape around my ruby
vial of blood and I leave knowing
the results as I walk toward
home, looking, like a man
for his keys, for anything
else, one more
image — maybe that old
car, its cushion sticking
from the bottom slit of the door,
caught like a tongue.

59

RECEIPT

Hang on to these. Someday
you may need them. Say you think
she looked at you like a god, that
dresses were orange, flowers yellow,
eyes blue grass green gazebo
white brass band red. Or when
exactly was it? Then, you say, no,
Sunday she says, so you find our
packet you have carefully saved,
Your Memories Enclosed. See?
It's the rolling-in clouds that
are yellow, your face green. Brass
flowers, she is blue. Red
lightning forks behind your
unfocused face, it's too dark,
some shadow gestures, which she turns
to touch like a god, you were old
and alone like you are now but don't
remember it that way, so you look
deep into the amber negatives for your
self. The squares are empty as Sunday morning.
Thank you for your order.

CONCENTRATION CAMP

I was hungry, we all were hungry,
the world was defined by hunger.
There was wire
round in our skulls
and coiled in stomachs.
They gave us something for the body,
our minds were worse.

In England
as I walked my fingers
brushed the bindings
which never seem to end.

Though sirens divide the night
my bed is empty
my body invisible
smiles at the black sentry.

What I learn
I let go
with the wind
and the wind goes over the wire.

THE WEANING

It starts with little things —
a blue web belt from the Navy,
a book of the greatest chess games,
a boy scout knife with ten blades.
You suspect that this time
they have not been lost, or mislaid, or left somewhere,
but subtracted, that something has begun
erasing,
like cyphers, like tracks,
the curios of your history
starting back at the first
and gaining on you every day.
When you begin to miss certain people,
you know the house itself is next
or the street of green trees.
One morning when you wake it will be
color
and you will wander for days in snow
before, suddenly, even the whiteness goes.
But by then it will be
just one more thing.